This book
belongs to

....

For Mum & Dad – C.C.
For Charlotte – T.v.R.

First published in Great Britain in 2017
by Fourth Wall Publishing
2 Riverview Business Park,
Shore Wood Road, Bromborough,
Wirral, Merseyside CH62 3RQ

Copyright©Fourth Wall Publishing 2017

ISBN: 978-1-910851-66-1

Printed in China.

**fourth wall
publishing**

Doctor James McGee
and the Time Machine

Written by **Chris Capstick**   Illustrated by **Tom van Rheenen**

Beneath the clouds of planet Earth,
In a house beside the sea,
There lives a rather special boy
Called Doctor James McGee.

His parents are both scientists –
Super intell-i-gent!
They love to spend time working on
Secret exper-i-ments.

Now as you may already know,
Young James loves science too.
He even has a PHD
In sticks and string and glue.

Then one bright and early morning,
As James drives into school,
A panicked dad calls from the lab,
"You'd better get here soon!"

"We have a huge emergency,
The time machine's gone mad!
It's acting totally crazy.
Oh, this is very bad!"

James reacts with lightning speed
And spins the car around.
He activates the turbo jets
Then launches off the ground!

They land the car outside the lab
And run in at full steam,
But as James steps in through the door
He's zapped by laser beams!

His parents shout and scream aloud
To warn their son to "STOP!"
But before they get their words out,
He's vanished with a 'POP!'

Then James zooms down a tube of light,
Rushing back through time.
He reappears high up a tree
Entangled in some vines!

From his amazing vantage point
Young James stares out in awe,
At fiery hot volcanoes
And lots of DINOSAURS!

The huge reptiles begin to run
Straight in his direction.
The ground begins to rumble,
It's a VOLCANIC ERUPTION!

James keeps his wits and has a think,
Then suddenly remembers –
His pockets full of rubber bands,
String and calculators!

He wriggles free and grabs the string
Then ties a big lasso.
As Tyrannosaurus Rex runs by,
He catches him, "WHOO HOO!"

James leaps aboard and reigns Rex in,
They race off in a flash,
Dodging lumps of molten rock,
Chunks of stone and ash.

Boiling lava rivers chase down
The rocky mountainside.
The red hot liquid closes in
And James must now decide!

He steers the mighty T-Rex
Towards the rugged coast.
They leap to safety just in time
Before they're turned to toast!

Below the swollen ocean waves
The whole world seems at peace,
Until the pair are swallowed by
A giant fishy beast!

The huge old fish swims on for days,
But then comes up for air,
So James and Rex both seize the chance
To escape their monstrous lair!

But where they are, they do not know,
The weather is sub-zero.
A blizzard howls and whips the snow,
Freezing our young hero.

In the end they're frozen stiff,
Forever intertwined.
How will poor frozen James escape
His journey back through time?

Back at the lab, his parents have
Both hardly stopped for food.
They work non-stop on the machine
So James can be rescued.

For days they toil without a break
With worry on their minds,
Until their friend comes running in,
Waving the news headlines...

INCREDIBLE DISCOVERY
FOUND FROZEN IN THE SNOW
A BOY RIDING A DINOSAUR FROM A ZILLION YEARS AGO!

So jumping in their flying car,
Both weeping tears of joy,
"The North Pole right away!" they say,
"Let's get our little boy."

Back at home the giant ice cube
Is melted to the floor,
And out comes Doctor James McGee
With his new pet dinosaur!